This ELMER book belongs to:

. . . .

Ⓐ

This paperback edition first published in 2009 by Andersen Press Ltd.
First published in Great Britain in 1999 by Andersen Press Ltd.,
20 Vauxhall Bridge Road, London SW1V 2SA.
Text and Illustration copyright © David McKee, 1999
The right of David McKee to be identified as the author and illustrator
of this work has been asserted by him in accordance with
the Copyright, Designs and Patents Act, 1988.
All rights reserved.
Colour separated in Switzerland by Photolitho AG, Zürich.
Printed and bound in China.

1   3   5   7   9   10   8   6   4   2

British Library Cataloguing in Publication Data available.

ISBN 978 1 84270 749 4

ELMER
and the Lost Teddy

David McKee

Andersen Press

The sky was already dark and full of stars when Elmer,
the patchwork elephant, heard the sound of crying.
It was Baby Elephant.
"He can't sleep," said Baby Elephant's mother.
"He wants his teddy. We took Teddy with us on a
picnic and somewhere we lost it."

"Never mind," said Elmer.
"I'll lend him my teddy. Tomorrow I'll look for the lost one."
Elmer went away and came back with his teddy. Baby Elephant smiled and was soon fast asleep with Elmer's teddy beside him.

The next day Elmer set off in search of the lost teddy.
He hadn't gone far when he met his cousin, Wilbur.
"Hello, Wilbur," said Elmer. "I'm looking for
Baby Elephant's lost teddy. Have you seen it?"
"No," said Wilbur. "But if I find it, I'll call you."

A little later a voice said, "Hello, Elmer. Where are you going?" It was Lion.

"Baby Elephant has lost his teddy and I'm looking for it," said Elmer.

"Oh dear," said Lion. "Baby Lion would be very upset if he lost his teddy. If I find it, I'll call you. Maybe Tiger has seen it."

As he came near Tiger's place, Elmer called out, "Yoho! Tiger!"
"Ssssh! Elmer," Tiger quietly called back. "The twins are asleep."
"Sorry," said Elmer. "Only, Baby Elephant has lost his teddy. Have you seen it?"
"That's serious," said Tiger. "The twins wouldn't sleep without their teddies. If I find it, I'll call you."

After that, Elmer visited the other animals.
All the young ones had their teddies, but none
of them had seen Baby Elephant's. They all said
the same thing, "If we find it, we'll call you."

It was getting late into the afternoon and Teddy was still lost. "I hope I find him soon," thought Elmer. "It's nearly night-time." It was at that moment that he heard a shout. "Help! Help!" And then again: "Help! I'm lost!"

Elmer pushed through some bushes and there
was a teddy bear. The voice came from the teddy.
"Please help me," said the teddy. "I'm lost. I want
Baby Elephant."
"You can talk," said Elmer in surprise.
"Please, take me home," said Teddy. "I can't
sleep without Baby Elephant."

Elmer still stared. "Your mouth isn't moving," he said.
Just then Wilbur appeared from the bushes.

"Wilbur," laughed Elmer. "I might have known it was you making Teddy speak."

Wilbur chuckled. "I said I'd call you if I found Teddy," he said. "And I did. Come on, let's take Teddy home, it's getting dark."

They set off together,
singing as they went.

Baby Elephant was excited to see his teddy
again and quickly gave back Elmer's teddy.

Baby Elephant's mother couldn't
thank Elmer and Wilbur enough.

"Elmer," said Wilbur, "weren't you worried that Baby
Elephant would want to keep your teddy? Your teddy is
very different; it's special."

"But, Wilbur, didn't you know?" said Elmer in surprise. "You don't have to be different to be special. All teddies are special, especially your own."